Haffert
First E:

Haffertee is a toy hamster. Ma Diamond made him for her little girl, Yolanda (usually known as Diamond Yo), when her pet hamster died.

In this book – the sixth in the Haffertee series – Haffertee gets his first taste of pancakes and hot cross buns. He nearly loses his friend Howl Owl. And he discovers how the baby born at Christmas grew up to be a King.

The charm of the stories lies in the funny, lovable character of Haffertee himself, and in the special place God has in the affections of Diamond Yo and her family.

The
Diamond
Family

Fran   Ma

Diamond Yo
with
Haffertee and
Howl Out

Pops

Mark

Chris.

Haffertee's
First Easter

Janet and John Perkins

A LION PAPERBACK

Oxford · Batavia · Sydney

Copyright © 1984 Janet and John Perkins
Illustrations copyright © 1984 Lion Publishing

Published by
Lion Publishing plc
Sandy Lane West, Littlemore, Oxford, England
ISBN 0 7459 1519 1
Lion Publishing Corporation
1705 Hubbard Avenue, Batavia, Illinois 60510, USA
ISBN 0 7459 1519 1
Albatross Books Pty Ltd
PO Box 320, Sutherland, NSW 2232, Australia
ISBN 0 7324 0026 0

First edition 1984
This edition 1989

Illustrations by Diane Matthes

Reproduced, printed and bound in Great Britain by
Hazell Watson & Viney Limited
Member of BPCC plc
Aylesbury, Bucks, England

Contents

It all began when Yo's pet hamster died. To cheer her up, Ma Diamond made a ginger-and-white toy hamster. The new Haffertee Hamster proved to be quite a character – inquisitive, funny and lovable. From his home in Yo's bedroom – shared with his friend Howl Owl and a strange collection of toys – he set out to explore Hillside House and meet the family: Ma and Pops Diamond and Yo's older brothers and sister, Chris, Fran and Mark. His adventures at home, at school and in the World Outside are told in six books of stories: *Haffertee Hamster, Haffertee's New House, Haffertee Goes Exploring, Haffertee's First Christmas, Haffertee Goes to School* and *Haffertee's First Easter*.

1

Not Just a Baby

The loft at Hillside House was full of people. Ma Diamond had declared the day a Spring Cleaning Day and all the family had to be there. They all were, and they were working hard.

All except Haffertee and Howl Owl. They were very busy . . . watching!

But not for long.

"Haffertee! Howl Owl! Don't just sit there," said Ma Diamond sternly. "Do something. See if you can sort out that box of Special People."

Now the Special People are usually kept in a green shoe-box near the top of the loft stairs. They are taken out very carefully at Christmas time to make a lovely crib-scene of the stable with Mary and Joseph and the animals.

Today they seemed to be all over the

place. Somebody must have knocked the box over.

Mary was under an old typewriter.

Joseph had fallen into a box of pencils.

Two of the angels were flat on their faces on top of a pile of comics. And the little donkey was upside down between two water pipes!

Haffertee and Howl Owl began to pick them all up carefully and put them back neatly into the shoe-box again.

It wasn't long before they were all safe and sound.

All except the little baby Jesus.

He wasn't anywhere around.

Haffertee struggled under Ma Diamond's old chair to look for him. Howl floated down into an empty box to look for him. And Mr Jumpastring hung about in a golf bag to see if he was there. But nobody could find the little baby Jesus. There was just no sign of him. No sign at all.

Until Diamond Yo started to look.

She found him almost at once in an old brown suitcase full of bits of broken dolls.

She picked him up very gently and carried him over to the shoe-box. She was just going to tuck him away in there when Haffertee started jumping and dancing about all over the place.

"Just a minute," he squeaked excitedly. "Let me have another look at him, please."

Yo hesitated for a moment and then put the little figure down on the floor in front of Haffertee.

"All right," she said firmly. "Just one last look and then he must go back."

Haffertee stood very still for some time, looking down at the baby. First this way, and then that way, and then the other way again. Then he began to nod his head and stroke his whiskers gently.

Yo knew what was coming. One of Haffertee's difficult questions. She could always tell.

"That's it, then," she said, all of a hurry, interrupting all that thinking and stroking and looking and nodding. "Away he goes!"

And she picked up the little baby Jesus and put him in the box.

Haffertee stood where he was for just a little while longer and then, very suddenly, he asked, "Will he be the same size next year?"

Diamond Yo nearly burst out laughing. But she managed to keep it down to a chuckle.

"Who? Jesus?" she asked, with a smile.

"Yes," said Haffertee, quite firmly. "Jesus. Will he be the same size next year?"

Yo swallowed and waited. She had to think this one out carefully because she knew Haffertee wanted a good answer.

"That little baby in the box will be the same size every year," she said at last. "We

13

always think about a little baby at Christmas time. But Jesus was not just a baby. He grew up, like little boys do."

Haffertee scratched a place behind his ear.

"Ah!" he said thoughtfully. "What did he grow up into?"

Yo thought about the next answer too, and then said, "He grew up to be a King in the end. Mr Jesus King."

"A King?" smiled Haffertee. "Mr Jesus King. That sounds great. I like that. Mr Jesus King. Yes. I like that very much."

He turned to go back down the loft ladder, and as he did so Diamond Yo began to sing, very softly at first but then much more loudly as Howl Owl and Haffertee joined in:

Jesus the baby was born in a stable
And grew up like little boys do.
Loved by his mother, his sisters
and brothers;
Playing around just like you.
He learned at his mother's knee
just what he had to be –
A King and a carpenter too.

Not just a baby.
Not just a schoolboy.
Not just a wonderful friend.
Not just a carpenter.
Not just a wandered.
He is a King in the end!

The whole family was singing away merrily before they got downstairs and Diamond Yo was delighted.

"That's one of Pops' songs," she said, happily. "We are going to sing it in church at Easter time."

Haffertee smiled.

"It certainly is a nice song," he said. "I'd like to try to learn it."

2

The Pancake Mixture

Soon after that Spring Cleaning Day in the loft, when all the Special People were put away, Ma Diamond started beating something in the kitchen.

Haffertee was upstairs in Diamond Yo's room trying to learn the words of Pops' Easter Song and he could hear the noise all the way up there.

"That noise needs looking into," he said quietly, to no one in particular. "It certainly needs looking into."

So he made his way carefully down the stairs and into the kitchen.

"Hello, Haffertee," said Ma Diamond, as soon as she saw who it was. "What can I do for you?"

"Nothing much," said Haffertee, shyly. "I heard you beating something down here when I was up in Yo's room and I thought I would like to see what is going on."

"Ah!" said Ma Diamond, wiping her hands on her apron. "I've been making a mixture. There! In that big red bowl. You can take a look if you like."

She lifted Haffertee up on to the shiny worktop and pointed him in the right direction. Then she went out of the back door to get the washing in.

Haffertee walked towards the big red bowl and tried very hard to take a look. But he couldn't. The edge of the bowl was much too high for that.

He walked round the bowl once, and then once again.

It was no good. He would have to jump for it.

He took a deep breath, bent his legs under him and then heaved himself up into the air. Up, and up, and up . . . down, and down, and down . . . SPLOSH! Right into a great yellow splodge.

He suddenly found himself surrounded by a thick sticky yellow mixture.

His hands were full of it.

His fur was clogged by it.

His ears were blocked by it.

He was very nearly right down under it.
"Oh! . . . Help! . . . HELP!"

Just in the nick of time, Ma Diamond
came back. She reached down and grabbed

him, lifting him up out of the bowl, all dripping and dribbling and oozing. She wiped off the worst of the mixture with her hands and then she put him gently down into a bowl of warm water in the sink.

Haffertee spluttered and splattered and splittered all over the place as Ma Diamond washed his fur and cleaned his ears and wiped his head. Then at last she set him down on a nice warm towel.

"There now," she said. "Just you sit there quietly for a while and dry off."

So Haffertee did. He sat there quite still and dried off. It was while he was drying off that he began to wonder about things.

"Whatever is that sticky yellow stuff?" he asked at last, nodding towards the big red bowl.

"That's my pancake mixture," said Ma Diamond, with a smile. "I had to make another lot."

"Pancake mixture," said Haffertee, curling his bottom lip. "Uggghh! What do you do with that?"

"We eat it," said Ma Diamond, beating the mixture a bit more with a big wooden spoon. "We cook it, we toss it in the air once or twice, we roll it up with lemon juice and sugar . . . and then we eat it!"

Haffertee made a very funny face. He couldn't think why anyone would want to eat that sticky mixture, nor why they should throw it in the air – unless it was to get rid of it. But he watched with great interest as Ma Diamond poured some of it into a hot pan on the stove.

She let it sizzle for a little while and then

tossed it up in the air.

Haffertee ducked. He felt quite sure that it was all coming down on his head. But it didn't. It came down, nicely turned, into the hot pan again and Ma let it sizzle for a few more minutes.

Then, out onto the plate came the pancake, and Ma Diamond quickly sprinkled it with lemon juice and sugar and rolled it up.

"Here," said Ma Diamond. "Try some."

Haffertee wasn't too sure about eating that sticky stuff. But he did, and it tasted great.

He liked it so much that he asked for some more.

He was just about to ask for a third helping when Diamond Yo came bursting in from playing with her friends.

"Mmmmmmm!" she shouted. "Pancake

Day. Yummy! Yummy! Can I have one now?"

"All right," said Ma. "Just wait a minute."

More of the yellow mix went into her pan. Sizzle! Sizzle! Sizzle! Up into the air a couple of times and then on with the lemon juice and sugar.

Diamond Yo was eating a lovely hot pancake in next to no time at all.

Haffertee watched her for a little while. Then he asked, "Why do we have pancakes today?"

Diamond Yo stopped eating and licked her lips.

"Because we like them," she said loudly. "And because today is Shrove Tuesday. Tomorrow Lent begins – and that reminds us that Easter is coming."

Haffertee liked the sound of those last words.

"Easter is coming," he said, his eyes growing wide. "Pancakes remind us that Easter is coming. What is so special about Easter?"

"Er . . . Weller," said Diamond Yo slowly, sounding just like their friend Howl

Owl. "You remember that at Christmas time we were all thinking about the little baby Jesus?"

Haffertee nodded. He remembered that well. He had had a great time being a Christmas Detective.

"Weller . . ." said Yo again. "At Easter time we think about what happened to Jesus when he grew up."

Haffertee nodded again. He stroked his whiskers gently and turned to go upstairs.

"What did happen to Mr Jesus King when he grew up?" he asked. "Did he eat pancakes?"

Ma Diamond nearly dropped her spoon.

Yo went quite red trying to hold in a loud laugh.

Haffertee didn't seem to notice, though, and made his way slowly back to Diamond Yo's room.

He was thinking about the pancake mixture and just beginning to wonder what other strange things he might be getting into at Easter time.

He felt sure there was a lot more to come.

And he was quite right, because Easter is a very special time in the Diamond family.

3

Pussy Willow Time

The days went by. Easter came closer and closer. But nothing much had happened since Haffertee had jumped into the pancake mixture. When was he going to learn some more about Mr Jesus King?

Then, one Saturday morning at breakfast, he heard something that made his whiskers tingle.

Pops Diamond had opened his big Bible and was reading aloud a most exciting story. It was all about Jesus riding into a place called Jerusalem on a donkey.

"The people were so pleased to see Jesus," Pops said, "that they broke off branches from the palm trees and put them on the dusty road in front of him. Some of them even put their coats on the road as well. There were great crowds of people – everyone singing and dancing and clapping

24

and shouting 'Long live the King!'"

Haffertee pricked up his ears. This was something new and it sounded good.

"A King riding on a donkey!" he said with a smile. "Are you sure?"

"Quite sure," said Pops Diamond firmly. "Jesus came as the King of Peace. We shall hear a lot more about that in church tomorrow, because it's Palm Sunday."

Haffertee sat quite still for a moment. He was thinking about Mr Jesus King riding that donkey into Jerusalem city.

His thoughts were interrupted by Ma Diamond getting up from the table.

"Right then," she said quickly. "Let's get all these breakfast things cleared and washed up. Then we can go to Pottinger Wood to get some pussy willow."

A strange expression crossed Haffertee's face. Pussy willow? Whatever was that? Was it something to do with the Purrswell kittens? There was no time to ask. Everyone was busy getting ready.

Pottinger Wood was not far away. It was a lovely sunny day and the birds were singing, happy that winter was over. Everything seemed fresh and new and bursting with

life. Fran and Yo ran over to a big bush full of furry grey bobbles.

"There's some lovely pussy willow here," they called, and began to pick the branches carefully.

So that's it, thought Haffertee.

Yes, those fat grey bobbles were as soft as the Purrswell kittens' fur. It was a good name.

It was fun in the wood, and they all enjoyed the walk. When they got home Ma Diamond arranged the pussy willow in some large vases and stood one of them on the window-sill. It looked lovely in the sunlight.

But Haffertee was still puzzled.

"Why did we have to go and pick that pussy willow today?" he burst out at last.

For once it was Chris who answered.

"Palm trees only grow in hot countries," he said, "so we pick pussy willow instead to remind us of the palms those people brought for Jesus."

Haffertee quickly snatched a pussy willow branch from the vase and began to wave it round and round his head in excitement. Chris had to duck to avoid being poked in the eye!

"Do you think Jesus is a King then?" Haffertee asked.

He didn't wait for an answer. He set off with his "palm branch" at top speed along the window-sill, waving it wildly all over the place.

There was a sudden movement from Pops' chair. Haffertee was getting rather too close to his nose!

"Yes," said Pops certainly. "I do think that Jesus is a King! In fact, I know he is."

Haffertee smiled, nodded and clambered down from the window-sill. He was going upstairs to Yo's room to tell all his toy cupboard friends about Mr Jesus King and the donkey and the branches of palm.

Howl Owl was there and a great crowd of toys. Haffertee told them the story Pops had read that morning. And when he had finished they gave a great cheer.

Then they all fetched branches of pussy willow and began to wave them in the air. Haffertee was persuaded to take a ride on

Rabbearmonklio's back and they made a wonderful procession round the room, shouting and clapping and singing a new verse of Pops Diamond's Easter Song.

He rode a young donkey right into the city
While hundreds of people were there.
Shouting and singing and clapping and dancing
And waving great palms in the air.
All those supporters, their sons and their daughters
Were saying, "The new King is here!"
Were saying, "The new King is here!"
Not just a baby.
Not just a schoolboy.
Not just a wonderful friend.
Not just a carpenter.
Not just a wanderer.
He is a King in the end!

At last the waving and the dancing and the singing stopped. Howl Owl smiled his slow smile.

"Weller," he said, in his very deepest voice. "You are learning a lot, Haffertee. And there's more to come."

4

Just Monday

The pussy willow march was over.

Palm Sunday – like all Sundays – had been great fun.

There were crowds of people at church and the story of Jesus riding into Jerusalem on a donkey had been exciting. Pops' Easter Song sounded great.

Now it was . . . just Monday and Yo was feeling YUCKY!!

There was an unusual hush in her room. Everyone was just waiting around for something to happen.

It was Yo who happened something.

"I know," she said, all of a sudden. "We'll explore the garage. There are lots and lots of things to find and play with in there."

"Great Idea," said Howl Owl in his very deep voice. "Great Idea." (He usually said everything twice.)

"I love exploring," said Mr Jumpastring, bouncing about merrily on his black elastic.

"You are clever, Yo," squeaked Haffertee. "Yes. Let's go and explore the garage."

So off they went together down to the garage.

Rabbearmonklio soon found a hammer and some nails and started banging them into everything.

Mr Jumpastring swung into action straight away – and knocked over a tin of red paint. It began to drip all over everything.

Howl Owl managed to fix the hose on to the tap – and turned it on. He showered everything!

Haffertee climbed on to a shelf and knocked a pile of empty cans all over the floor. They clanged and clattered everywhere.

Yo found an old pillow and began whirling it above her head. It suddenly burst wide open and scattered feathers all around.

In no time at all, Just Monday was Fun Monday!

In the middle of all the excitement Chris Diamond came into the garage to get a saw.

He was putting up some shelves in the kitchen for Ma Diamond.

He couldn't see for feathers and showers!

For a moment he just stood there trying to work out what was going on. Then he grabbed a broom and charged in.

"Out! Out! Out!" he shouted and began to shoo them off.

Yo and the others were not very pleased. They were having great fun and Chris was spoiling it.

They began to hiss and boo and shout all sorts of names at him. But it didn't seem to make any difference. He just kept shooing them off.

He was very angry.

"This is Pops' workshop," he shouted. "Just look at the mess you have made of it. Out! Out! Out!"

Yo turned and ran out of the garage. She just managed to avoid the broom.

The others followed her just as quickly. They made their way up into Diamond Yo's room and sat there wondering what would happen next.

They heard Chris moving about down below and then they heard the car. Pops was home. Now for it!

They hardly dared to breathe.

There were footsteps on the stairs. Pops was coming up.

The door opened slowly and there he was . . . with a very angry Chris just behind him, still holding the broom.

Pops looked sternly at each one of them. The silence seemed to last for ever.

"You really are very naughty," he said at last. "Very naughty indeed. Not only have

you made a dreadful mess in the garage but
you have also been very rude to Chris . . .
Now what are you going to do about it?"

There was no sound.

Haffertee looked at Yo. Yo looked at
Howl Owl. Howl Owl looked at Rabbear-
monklio. Rabbearmonklio looked at Mr
Jumpastring and Mr Jumpastring looked at
Haffertee.

It was Howl Owl who spoke first.

"Er . . . sorry," he said slowly. "Er . . .
sorry."

"Yes," said Haffertee in a whisper.
"Sorry, Pops."

Diamond Yo took a very deep breath.

"I'm sorry we made such a mess of the
garage," she said quickly. "It was really my
fault. And I'm sorry we were so rude to you,
Chris."

It was all said in a great hurry but Pops knew she meant it.

He smiled and nodded. Chris smiled too.

"Right," said Pops. "You can clear it all up this afternoon!" He turned to go, then suddenly thought of something.

"Do you know what all this reminds me of?" he said, as he turned back.

Haffertee and the others tried hard to think. But making a dreadful mess in the garage and being rude to Chris didn't remind them of anything.

"Well, I'll tell you, then," said Pops, when no answer came. "It reminds me of what happened at the Temple in Jerusalem."

Haffertee lifted his head. He was listening very carefully now. Was this something new about Easter?

"Er . . . Did the feathers fly about in there, too?" he asked.

"Not quite like they did in the garage," said Pops. "But the doves must have fluttered around a bit."

"Of course," said Yo quickly. "Of *course*! I remember now. Jesus drove the traders out of the Temple. They were selling sheep and

35

goats and doves – and cheating people of their money. Jesus told them God's Temple was meant to be a quiet place of prayer but they were making it a robbers' den. He really upset a lot of people that day and they all turned against him."

Haffertee looked at Yo carefully. He was very puzzled.

"Turned against Mr Jesus King?" he said slowly. "After all that fun on Palm Sunday!"

Pops smiled.

"Yes," he said. "It does sound strange, doesn't it? But crowds can be like that."

Haffertee frowned.

"Easter!" he said. "Easter sounds a bit strange to me."

5

The Purrswell Kittens and the Flowerpot

Haffertee was sitting quietly on Diamond Yo's desk. He was looking out of the window at the back garden. Tina and Smudge, the two Purrswell kittens, were playing about on the stone steps up by the raspberry canes, very close to a large flowerpot.

It was full of lovely flowers.

Ma Diamond had been talking about them at breakfast. She had kept them carefully in the house from Christmas time. Now she had put them out of doors to give them some fresh air and sunlight.

Suddenly the flowerpot began to move. The Purrswell kittens were playing much too close.

The pot went this way, and that way, and this way again. Now up and down. Round and round . . . wibbling and wobbling and . . . falling.

Roly-poly right down the steps.

It crashed from the top of the steps to the bottom. Clatter! Bounce! Splat!

Bits of flowerpot flew in all directions.

Dirt scattered all over the place.

The beautiful flowers flopped out on the ground. They did look sorry for themselves.

Tina and Smudge stopped jumping about and looked at the mess. Then they walked down the steps and sniffed at everything.

They tried to make the flowerpot jump by poking it with their paws.

When nothing happened they gave up and scuttled into the house. Haffertee heard the cat-door rattle as they came in.

Just a few moments later, Ma Diamond went out into the garden to put some rubbish in the bin. She saw the broken pot and the scattered dirt and drooping flowers.

"Whatever has happened?" she shouted. "Just look at this mess!"

She bent down and picked up the flowers and brought them inside. Then she began to ask all the family about the mess.

No one seemed to know anything about it – least of all the Purrswell kittens.

"I have been playing with the puppy next

door," said Tina, when Ma asked her what she knew. "But I did see Haffertee out there just after breakfast."

"It wasn't me," said Smudge, just as firmly. "I've been talking to Jeremy Tom for the past half-hour and I didn't hear anything at all. I saw Haffertee going out there, though!"

Haffertee gulped and blinked his eyes and shook his head. He just couldn't believe his ears.

He hadn't heard anyone tell lies like that before.

It wasn't very long before Ma Diamond did something about it.

"Haffertee," she called rather roughly. "Just come here a minute, will you?"

Haffertee did as he was told. He wasn't too sure about what was going to happen.

He soon found out.

Ma Diamond was very angry about the broken pot and the drooping flowers, and she said so.

She blamed Haffertee for it all.

Haffertee just stood there with a large lump bobbling in his throat and a big tear trickling from one eye. He just couldn't

believe it. He was amazed. It wasn't fair! It wasn't true. He had only been sitting there watching!

It was a very sad Haffertee who stumbled up to Diamond Yo's room after that scolding.

Yo was tidying some books when Haffertee came in.

"Hello!" she said. "What's up with you?" Haffertee didn't think that she really wanted to know because she went on tidying the books and didn't even turn round again.

He found it hard to make his voice work properly. But at last he managed to tell her what had happened.

"Oh, Haffertee," she said quickly. "You really should be more careful!"

Haffertee didn't know what to do. He

felt like shouting at the top of his voice . . .
"I DIDN'T DO IT!" But instead he just sat
there on the desk getting sadder and sadder.

It was Pops Diamond who discovered the
truth when he came in later. He could be a
very good listener sometimes, and he soon
found out what had really happened.

He lifted Haffertee up in the air and
stroked his head and tickled his neck.

Haffertee smiled a bit and then began to
feel much better. Now he knew that somebody believed him.

"You know, Haffertee," said Pops Diamond slowly. "We're thinking a lot about
Jesus this week. And it was a bit like this for
him."

Haffertee turned sharply. He was suddenly all ears again.

"You mean he had trouble with the Purrswell kittens, too?" Pops laughed out loud.

"No, Haffertee," he chuckled at last. "Not quite like that. But soon after Palm Sunday when everyone welcomed him as King, they all turned against him."

Haffertee was very quiet.

"And did they get him into trouble too?" Pops was very careful with his answer.

"Yes Haffertee, they did," he said slowly. "There was so much trouble that the soldiers made him a prisoner. Two people told dreadful lies about him and all his friends ran away."

Haffertee shuddered and drew in a sharp breath.

"I'm so glad you didn't run away," he said softly. "I really needed you."

Pops felt lovely and warm inside. Haffertee did say the nicest things!

6

Going . . .
to Come Back

It was Thursday morning – Maundy Thursday, Yo said. Haffertee was sitting on the window-sill listening to Yo reading the story about Mr Jesus King having supper with his special friends and saying Goodbye.

"I have to go away and you can't come with me," Yo read. Haffertee was all ears. Why did Mr Jesus King have to leave his friends and make them sad?

It was at that very moment that the rumbling began. Rumbling and tumbling and jumbling . . . up in the loft. Someone was up there, making a terrible noise.

Haffertee looked at the ceiling and frowned.

"Whatever is that?" he asked in surprise.

"That's Fran," said Yo. "She's looking for a suitcase."

"Looking for a suitcase," stuttered

44

Haffertee. "Whatever does she want a suit-case for?"

Yo put the Bible down carefully on her desk.

"She's going away today," she said slowly and rather sadly, "to see some friends of hers. There are three children and their mother is ill in hospital. Fran's going to help look after them."

Haffertee sat still for a moment. He didn't like to think of Fran going away. She wouldn't be at home for Easter.

It was then that the idea came. Haffer-tee's ideas come and go very quickly and none of them stays very long. This one got out immediately.

"If Fran is going away today we ought to have a GOODBYE PARTY for her."

Yo looked at him in surprise. His eyes were wide and his smile was broad. Haffertee and parties thought a lot of each other!

"A party?" she said, with something of a frown. "A party? Here?"

"Well, yes," said Haffertee quickly. "In my Very Own Box."

Yo turned and looked at Haffertee's Very Own Box in the corner. It looked very small indeed. She went on looking at the box and thinking about Haffertee's idea for ages.

"Why not," she burst out at last. "Why ever not! But I don't think we shall all get in there. Perhaps you would like to use my room?"

Haffertee jumped up and down three times and then turned round twice. He was delighted.

"Oh thank you, Yo!" he shouted. "Thank you very much."

So Fran's GOODBYE PARTY was quickly arranged and Yo's room rearranged so that all the family could get in. The bed went against the wall and lots of cushions

46

came in to be sat on. Yo made banana sandwiches and jellies, and there were sweets and nuts and ice creams for everybody – all set out nicely on a big coloured tablecloth.

Ma Diamond brought in a very special cake just before Pops said "Thank You" to God for all the food. She put it down very gently.

"This is a Fran cake," she said when Pops had finished, and she winked at Haffertee.

Haffertee began to think about that sticky yellow mix he had jumped into. The cake didn't look much like that.

"No, Haffertee," said Ma, "– a Francake not a pancake. And no one's to throw it up in the air!"

Haffertee smiled.

Fran was very pleased with her cake.

The party helped to make them all feel better about Fran going away. Everyone did their best to cheer the others up.

Pops Diamond sang a song about a Music Man from Abercrombie.

Haffertee did a splendid dance on the window-sill, while Chris played a tune on his tin whistle.

Mark stood on his head against the wall!

Even some of Mr Jumpastring's terrible jokes were really funny.

But when the fun time was over everyone was suddenly quiet.

"Let's sing another verse of Pops' Easter Song," Yo said. Fran picked up her guitar and started strumming away softly. Yo began to sing and all the rest joined in.

Just near the end, when he had all his friends
Around him to share in a meal,
He started to tell them he just had to leave them.
Imagine the way they would feel!
But when he had gone he would come back again
And be with them always for real!
Not just a baby.
Not just a schoolboy.
Not just a wonderful friend.
Not just a carpenter.
Not just a wanderer.
He is a King in the end!

Fran waited for a moment or so when the

song was over and then put down the guitar.

"Thank you all very much," she said softly. "It's been a lovely party and I have enjoyed it. I shall miss you all on Easter Sunday morning when you sing all those wonderful songs."

Haffertee thought about Fran going away for Easter. He didn't like the idea at all and he said so, sadly.

Fran listened and then gave him a special hug.

"Don't worry, Haffertee," she said gently. "I'm going to come back!"

Haffertee's eyes brightened at that and he began to stroke his whiskers.

"Did Jesus go to come back?" he asked at last.

Fran smiled. "Yes," she said firmly. "He did."

"Ah!" said Haffertee happily. "That's all right then."

7

Good Friday's Bad!

On Good Friday morning Ma Diamond was very busy buttering hot cross buns as fast as she could go.

Pops Diamond had been up very early to fetch them from the baker just up the hill, and now the whole family was enjoying eating them.

"Why are they called hot cross buns?" asked Haffertee between munches.

"Because they are hot, to start with," said Ma Diamond with a smile. "And because they have this very special sign on them." She bent down with a bun in her hand and showed Haffertee the cross marked on top.

"It's a sign that says GOD LOVES US," she said softly.

"Oh," said Haffertee. "How can it say that?"

"Well," said Pops Diamond as he put down his second bun, "today is called Good Friday. It's the day when we remember that God loved us so much he sent his Son Jesus into our world to give up his life for us. Although he'd done nothing wrong he was tried and condemned to death. Soldiers nailed him to a wooden cross and left him there to die."

"Left the King to die?" said Haffertee in surprise, not really believing his own ears. "Didn't anyone try to help him?"

Pops Diamond looked very ashamed.

"No, I'm afraid not," he said. "Jesus' mother was there all the time, loving him. But she couldn't do much about it. Most of his friends had run away because they were scared."

Haffertee stood there frowning, thinking about all those people who just let Jesus die. And he began to get very angry.

"Good Friday is Bad!" he muttered through tight lips. "Good Friday is BAD."

"Haffertee's right," said Diamond Yo, nibbling the last crumb of her hot cross bun. "Good Friday is bad. It was bad for Jesus but it was good for us."

She gave Haffertee a comforting squeeze.

"It sounds funny, Haffertee, but Jesus had to die. At least, *someone* had to. It was either him or us . . . We really deserved it. But he died instead. So it was bad for Jesus — but it was good for us, because now we can be God's friends. So it really is Good Friday!"

Haffertee was quiet for a moment as he thought about that. Then he stood up.

"I'm going out into the garden," he said briskly. "I need some fresh air. These hot cross buns are making me feel sad."

And he wandered off into the garden and up to the rhubarb patch where he had once hidden from the Spotted Dog. He stood there for a long time.

Suddenly he heard some very strange struggling noises. It was Samson the tortoise – and he was upside down. He was twisting and kicking and trying very hard to turn over. It was no use, though. He wasn't getting anywhere on his own. Haffertee moved over to him quickly and began to push hard on one side of the shell. He grunted and groaned. He moved his feet about to get a better push, and at long last, with a great shuddering thump, Samson turned right way up again.

He nodded his head at Haffertee, said "Thank you" and then plodded off slowly into the long grass.

Haffertee just stood there, puffed out!

He was very surprised when he heard Yo speaking behind him. She had crept out to see what was going on.

"Well done, Haffertee," she said. "Well done! You saw Samson in trouble and you helped him. That's what Jesus wants his friends to do. He tells us in the Bible that when we help someone in trouble, he is just as happy as if we had done it for him."

Haffertee stood there, breathing heavily, for quite some time.

"Come on," he said at last. "Let's go back to the kitchen." They set off down the garden steps together. He was thinking hard all the way.

When they arrived in the kitchen he said, "Does Jesus have lots of helpful friends, then?"

"Oh yes," said Yo quickly. "Lots and lots."

Haffertee reached for another hot cross bun.

"And will they all be eating hot cross buns today?" he asked.

Yo laughed.

"No. Not all of them," she said. "But they will all be thinking of him. This is a special cross day, you know."

Haffertee finished his mouthful.

"I do wish I'd been there," he said, still thinking about Jesus all alone. "I would have helped him somehow!"

"Good old Haffertee," said Yo kindly,

stroking his head gently. Deep down inside she knew that Jesus had had to die. No one could have helped him. That was the bad news. But then from the same deep down inside a chuckle came.

"But after Friday," she told Haffertee firmly, "there is always Sunday morning!"

Haffertee smiled. He didn't quite understand what Yo was talking about, but he wouldn't have long to wait now to find out.

8

Pieces of Howl

Something was very wrong.

Haffertee had a strange feeling inside.

He couldn't think what it was at first but then all at once he knew.

Howl Owl was missing!

He hadn't come in for any of the hot cross buns and he wasn't anywhere around the house. The shelf above the door in Yo's room was empty. Haffertee began to ask a few questions.

Diamond Yo said she had seen him going down to the kitchen.

Ma Diamond said she had seen him talking to the Purrswell kittens.

The Purrswell kittens said they had seen him going up to the top of the garden.

There was no sign of Howl Owl at the top of the garden, so Haffertee decided to go and look in the wilderness.

He found William the donkey up there, on the grassy patch under the beech tree.

"Hee Haw Hallo!" he called, when he saw Haffertee coming. "How are you?"

"Very well, thank you," said Haffertee, as cheerfully as he could. He wasn't really feeling very well at all. There was a sick hollow in his tummy.

"Have you seen Howl Owl at all this morning?" he asked politely.

William nodded his head towards a path that led up the hill to an old ruined cottage.

"I saw him very early this morning, skimming along up there," he said.

Haffertee was beginning to get very anxious and he set off quickly up the path without even saying thank you.

William didn't seem to notice. He returned to crunching thistles.

The path beyond the grassy patch was all new to Haffertee. He hadn't been that way before and it did look rather frightening. He gritted his teeth, swallowed a fear or two, and hurried on. He wanted to find Howl Owl.

What he found up there in the ruined cottage was very, very sad.

He found . . . not Howl, but *pieces* of Howl.

His wings were under a stone.

His body was dangling from a broken shelf.

And his stuffing was all over the place.

There could be no doubt about it.

Howl Owl was dead.

Haffertee just stood there and sobbed. He had never seen anything like it. Who could have done such a cruel thing?

Haffertee did not know. All he knew was that his dear, dear friend Howl Owl was dead.

At last, when there were no more sobs left, he collected all the bits of his friend together and half-carried, half-dragged them down the hill, past William, through the bramble tunnel, round past the nettle patch, through the hole in the fence and down the garden steps to Hillside House.

He was tired out when he got to the back door.

He knocked wearily.

Diamond Yo opened the door.

When she saw Haffertee and the pieces

of Howl she let out a loud cry and the tears began to run down her cheeks on to her green dress.

She lifted Haffertee up with the pieces of Howl and held them both very close.

Ma Diamond suddenly appeared from the kitchen.

"Whatever is the matter?" she asked. "Why are you crying?"

Then she saw the pieces of Howl.

"Oh!" was all she could say.

Slowly and sadly the three of them walked upstairs to Diamond Yo's room. They put the terrible bundle of torn Howl on to the bed and just sat there together.

Haffertee said nothing.

Diamond Yo said nothing.

Ma Diamond said nothing.

There was just nothing to say.

Life in the Diamond family would never be the same again.

It was a very sad Haffertee and Diamond Yo who went to bed that night. God didn't seem to be very nice at all. They didn't say any prayers.

Neither of them slept much, either.

They just lay there, thinking about the

wonderful times they had had together with Howl Owl.

Morning came slowly and smiled at them through the curtains. Saturday always seemed to come in smiling.

But there was no one on the shelf above the door.

"Good morning, Haffertee! Good morning, Yo!" said a surprisingly cheerful voice. "Look what I've got!"

The two of them turned round slowly – and looked.

Then they both shot out of bed.

They simply could not believe their eyes.

There was Ma Diamond holding a very familiar figure in her arms. It was Howl Owl.

He was all put together again.

His eyes were bright and shining and his black beak was gleaming. He was as fat as ever. He was alive and real and himself again.

Haffertee and Diamond Yo were absolutely amazed and delighted.

"However did you do it?" asked Diamond Yo.

"Yes," chirped Haffertee. "However did

you do it?"

"Weller . . ." said Ma Diamond in a deep voice, trying to sound like Howl Owl, and smiling merrily.

"Weller . . . I made him in the first place, didn't I? So I made him again. I spent a lot of last night putting him all together again – and here he is!"

"Yes. Here I jolly well am," said Howl Owl in his deepest voice ever. "Here I jolly well am!"

"Oh Howl!" shouted Haffertee, with a lovely warm feeling coming up from his toes all the way to his ears. "Oh Howl!"

He rushed over to his big barn owl friend and hugged him as tight as he could. (It wasn't very tight, because Howl was so far round.) Howl lifted one of his wings and rested it gently on Haffertee's shoulders.

They stood there together for a long time.

Everything was all right again now.

Ma Diamond had worked a miracle!

9

The Easter Day
Egg Hunt

It was Easter Sunday. But it was still dark
and no one in the Diamond Family seemed
to know very much about it!

They were all fast asleep.

The alarm clock went on clanging and
clanging for a long time before Pops Diamond reached out to switch it off. It was
very early indeed. But no one could go back
to sleep. Not if they were to get down to
Black Rock Point in time for the special
Sunrise Service.

It was all a great rush and scramble, but
somehow they made it.

They joined a big crowd of people all
singing together and saying THANK YOU
for Jesus being alive on Easter Day. As they
sang, the sky grew light and the sun came
up, glowing red.

Back at Hillside House afterwards, it was

breakfast and hot drinks for everyone. The wind on the Point had been very cold.

Haffertee sat on the kitchen table, impatiently waiting for the Easter Day Egg Hunt to begin.

Diamond Yo had told him all about it. And now that the day had arrived Haffertee was very anxious to get on with it.

Pops Diamond had hidden some pieces of card around the house, and each card had a big bright yellow letter written on it. If you could find all the cards and then unscramble the letters properly . . . you would know where to find the chocolate Easter eggs.

Haffertee wanted to find them as soon as possible.

He had arranged to go round the house with Yo because he was sure that some of the cards would be in places he could not possibly reach.

So together they searched and searched.

Pops had hidden fifteen cards, and Haffertee and Yo managed to find five of them.

There was an L behind the television set.

There was an H stuck underneath the

kitchen table.

There was a G in a pile of newspapers and a T in the toy cupboard.

The hardest one of all was another H, in Diamond Yo's pillowcase, only much further down than Haffertee ever went.

It was great fun searching, and even more fun trying to work out what all the letters said.

Everyone put the cards they had found on the kitchen table. Then they sat down together to think.

They moved this one there, and that one here, and others all round, until at last they had it.

HOLE IN THE GROUND

"Hole in the ground!" said Haffertee in surprise. "But where?" He really was in a hurry to find the eggs.

Pops smiled as he explained that the HOLE IN THE GROUND was in the garden under the holly bush.

There was a rush for the door.

In the garden under the holly bush was a round stone about the size of Howl Owl. Chris moved it carefully to one side and . . .

There they were! – a feast of lovely

chocolate eggs all neatly covered with sparkling coloured foil and nestling on a piece of soft white cloth.

Haffertee gave a great whoop of delight . . . and nearly fell into the hole!

Diamond Yo held on to him very firmly as she bent down to pick up the eggs. Then she gave them out. There was one for everyone.

When they were all back in the kitchen, Haffertee began to tear at the foil on his egg, scattering it everywhere. He just couldn't wait.

"Hold on a minute, Haffertee," said Yo. "Don't throw litter about like that. Here, put it in this," and she held out a wastepaper basket.

Haffertee gathered up all the foil and

threw it in. Then he began to eat his egg with great pleasure.

He was soon very sticky and covered in chocolate. As he sat there, licking his lips and trying to unstick his hands, he frowned a little.

"Why do we have chocolate eggs on Easter Sunday, then?" he asked, all of a sudden. "What have eggs got to do with Mr Jesus King?"

Yo looked at Pops and smiled. They had been expecting something like this.

"Well," said Yo slowly, "it's what's hidden inside the egg that matters. Every baby bird starts life inside an egg – and when the chick pecks its way out of the shell, that's a new life beginning."

Haffertee nodded, but he was still frowning.

Yo knew there were more questions to come.

"Was Jesus inside an egg, then?" he asked.

"Not an egg, Haffertee," said Pops, chuckling.

Ma Diamond joined in. "You remember Good Friday?" she said.

Haffertee nodded and licked his lips again. He was thinking about the hot cross buns with butter.

"When Jesus died," Ma said, "they buried him in a cave – a hole in the ground. And on Easter morning God let him out. Jesus was alive again. That's what's so special about Easter!"

Haffertee stood up straight and still.

"You mean God put Jesus all together again?" he spluttered in amazement. "God did a miracle with Mr Jesus King just like you did with Howl Owl?"

Ma Diamond smiled.

"Why yes, Haffertee. You could say that."

"Then I *will* say that," said Haffertee with a grin. "I certainly will." He brushed his front fur carefully and spoke in a very loud voice. "God did a miracle with Mr Jesus King just like the one Ma Diamond did with Howl Owl! Mr Jesus King came alive again." His voice squeaked a bit with excitement as he added, "Good Friday is Bad, but Easter Sunday is Good!"

Pops picked Haffertee up gently.

"That's the truth of it, Haffertee," he said.

Haffertee snuggled down into Pops' hand.

"There is something very special about Mr Jesus King," he said merrily. "Something very special indeed."

Yo nodded.

Haffertee was right again.

10
King of Hearts

Soon after dinner on Easter Sunday Haffertee began to do some rather strange things.

First he went up into the loft to get some white card.

Then he went into his Very Own Box in the corner of Diamond Yo's room and shut the door behind him very carefully.

He stayed there for most of the afternoon and strange noises and singing came from inside.

When he came out at last there was a slight smile on his face. He looked quite pleased with himself.

Next he went into the garage and found a small trowel.

He went to the place under the holly bush where Pops had hidden the Easter eggs and began to look for something.

There were no more eggs. But the stone

Chris had moved was still there. So was the hole.

Haffertee began to call someone's name.

There was no reply. Whoever he was calling didn't seem to hear. So he began to dig.

He dug and dug and dug, until he disappeared right into the hole.

Just at that very moment Diamond Yo came into the garden. All she could see were clouds of dirt flying up into the air and landing in a pile beside the hole in the ground under the holly bush.

She moved closer to see what was going on. When she saw who was in the hole she was very surprised. She was even more surprised when she saw what he was doing.

"Haffertee," she called loudly. "Whatever are you doing down there?"

Haffertee stopped digging and leaned on his trowel. He seemed a bit uncertain.

"I'm looking for Mr Jesus King," he said at last.

"Looking for Mr Jesus King?" said Yo in surprise. "Down there? You're looking for Mr Jesus King?"

Haffertee didn't really see the sense of

saying things over and over again. But perhaps Yo had not had time to wash her ears
properly in all that rush and hurry to get to
the Sunrise Service that morning.

So he said once more, "Yes. I'm looking
for Mr Jesus King."

Yo's mouth dropped wide open.

"Oh!" she said. "Er . . . Oh . . . Are
you? But why are you looking down there?"

Haffertee made an impatient sort of
clucking noise with his tongue. Perhaps

Easter Sunday was a Yo Being Difficult Day, he thought. But he didn't say so.

"Well," he said, "Ma Diamond told me this morning that God let Jesus out of a hole in the ground. This is the only hole in the ground that I knew. So I thought he might still be around somewhere."

And with that he turned back to his digging.

"Wait a minute," shouted Yo, trying desperately to keep out of the way of the dirt that flew up at her in showers.

"Wait a minute, Haffertee. He isn't there!"

Haffertee stopped digging once more and turned very slowly towards her. "All right," he said, rather fiercely. "So he isn't here. Then you just tell me where he is."

Yo swallowed hard. She wasn't really ready for that question.

There was a long silence as Haffertee waited for the answer and Yo struggled to find it.

"Jesus didn't go back to that cave," she said, "any more than a baby bird goes back inside its shell. He came alive and he stayed alive for ever. That's how we can know him now. But we don't see him. He's with everyone who loves him. He's" – and she smiled – "he's King of my heart."

It was Haffertee's turn to swallow hard. He was trying his best to understand.

"Oh!" was all he managed to say. "Then there isn't much sense in my going on digging in this hole, is there?"

Yo shook her head. Together the two of them filled up the hole and then went slowly up to Yo's room.

No word was spoken for a long time.

They just sat there together, quietly.

At last Haffertee sighed a great big sigh and went over to his Very Own Box. Yo thought he was going in there to cry because he was so disappointed. But when he came out again there was no sign of tears. He was smiling all over his face!

"Well, then," he said cheerfully, "you had better have this."

Yo looked at what Haffertee was holding.

It was a crown . . . a lovely coloured crown with golden sparkle all over it, and the words MR JESUS KING in big red letters all round the edge. It was splendid.

Haffertee had made it beautifully.

"Oh Haffertee," said Yo, surprised again by her soft-toy friend. "You really are a smasher!"

Haffertee smiled back.

"Is he the King of Hearts, then?" he asked with a merry sparkle in his eye.

Yo chuckled for a moment and thought about an answer.

"Yes," she said firmly. "And the King of Diamonds, too!"

Then she softly hummed Pops Diamond's special Easter Song. When she got to the chorus Haffertee joined in:

> *Not just a baby.*
> *Not just a schoolboy.*
> *Not just a wonderful friend.*
> *Not just a carpenter.*
> *Not just a wanderer.*
> *He is a King in the end!*

Pops Diamond's Easter Song

Jesus the baby was born in a stable
And grew up like little boys do.
Loved by his mother, his sisters and brothers;
Playing around just like you.
He learned at his mother's knee
just what he had to be –
A King and a carpenter too.

> *Not just a baby.*
> *Not just a schoolboy.*
> *Not just a wonderful friend.*
> *Not just a carpenter.*
> *Not just a wanderer.*
> *He is a King in the end!*

He rode a young donkey right into the city
While hundreds of people were there.
Shouting and singing and clapping and dancing
And waving great palms in the air.

All those supporters,
their sons and their daughters
Were saying "The new King is here!"

> *Not just a baby.*
> *Not just a schoolboy.*
> *Not just a wonderful friend.*
> *Not just a carpenter.*
> *Not just a wanderer.*
> *He is a King in the end!*

Just near the end, when he had all his
friends
Around him to share in a meal,
He started to tell them he just had to leave
them.
Imagine the way they would feel!
But when he had gone he would come back
again
And be with them always for real!

> *Not just a baby.*
> *Not just a schoolboy.*
> *Not just a wonderful friend.*
> *Not just a carpenter.*
> *Not just a wanderer.*
> *He is a King in the end!*

Jesus from Galilee, dead as a man can be.
Stuck in a cave on his own.
Earthquake came suddenly, shaking things terribly.
God rolls away that great stone!
Out from the ground he came.
Jesus alive again.
Making the whole world his home.

> *Not just a baby.*
> *Not just a schoolboy.*
> *Not just a wonderful friend.*
> *Not just a carpenter.*
> *Not just a wanderer.*
> *He is a King in the end!*